Reeve Lindbergh

The Midnight Farm

paintings by Susan Jeffers

Dial Books for Young Readers · New York

For Jonny and for Jane, with love
R. L.

For Uncle Ralph and Aunt Claire
S. J.

Published by Dial Books for Young Readers
A Division of NAL Penguin Inc.
2 Park Avenue, New York, New York 10016

Published simultaneously in Canada
by Fitzhenry & Whiteside Limited, Toronto

Printed in U.S.A.
Design by Atha Tehon
First Edition
COBE
1 3 5 7 9 10 8 6 4 2

Library of Congress Cataloging-in-Publication Data
Lindbergh, Reeve. The midnight farm.
Summary: Secrets of the dark are revealed in
this poem describing a farm at midnight.
1. Night —Juvenile poetry. 2. Farm life —Juvenile poetry.
3. Children's Poetry, American. [1. Night —Poetry.
2. Farm Life —Poetry. 3. American poetry.]
I. Jeffers, Susan, ill. II. Title.
PS3552.R6975M5 1987   811'.54   86-1722
ISBN 0-8037-0331-7   ISBN 0-8037-0333-3 (lib. bdg.)

The illustrator wishes to extend her special
thanks to Carol and Misha Isaak.

The full-color artwork was prepared using a fine-line pen
with ink, dyes, and gouache. They were applied over
a detailed pencil drawing that was then erased.

Here is the dark when day is done,
Here is the dark with no moon or sun,
Here is the dark when all lights are out,
Here is the heart of the dark.

Here is the dark of the chair in the hall
Where one old dog curls up in a ball,

Breathing each breath with a rise and a fall
In the dark of the chair in the hall.

Here is the dark by the big wood stove
Where two white cats have a leftover glove

And a birthday card that was signed with love
In the dark by the big wood stove.

Here is the dark of the maple tree
Where a raccoon family, one, two, three,

Is making a home in a place that was free
In the dark of the maple tree.

Here is the dark by the barnyard gate
Where four farm geese are staying up late.

They know wild geese will come if they wait
In the dark by the barnyard gate.

Here is the dark of the stable door
Where five horses stamp their feet on the floor

And blow through their noses and stamp some more
In the dark of the stable door.

Here is the dark in the barn at night
Where six cows stand, all black and white.

Their heads are low and their eyes are bright
In the dark in the barn at night.

Here is the dark in back of the barn
Where seven fat sheep are keeping warm

On hay from the meadows surrounding the farm
In the dark in back of the barn.

Here is the dark where the chickens rest
Where eight little chicks have feathery breasts

And ruffled up shoulders and heads on their chests
In the dark where the chickens rest.

Here is the dark of the orchard pond
Where nine deer gather from all around

To drink at night without any sound
In the dark of the orchard pond.

Here is the dark of the old stone wall
Where ten small field mice scamper and call

While hiding the seeds and berries that fall
In the dark of the old stone wall.

Here is the dark of the midnight farm,
Safe and still and full and warm,

Deep in the dark and free from harm
In the dark of the midnight farm.